Published in the United States of America by The Child's World®
1980 Lookout Drive • Mankato, MN 56003-1705
800-599-READ • www.childsworld.com

ACKNOWLEDGMENTS
The Child's World®: Mary Berendes, Publishing Director
The Design Lab: Kathleen Petelinsek, Design and Page Production
Literacy Consultants: Cecilia Minden, PhD, and Joanne Meier, PhD

LIBRARY OF CONGRESS
CATALOGING-IN-PUBLICATION DATA
Moncure, Jane Belk.
  My "h" sound box / by Jane Belk Moncure ; illustrated by
Rebecca Thornburgh.
    p. cm. — (Sound box books)
  Summary: "Little h has an adventure with items beginning
with his letter's sound, such as a hen, a horse, a hog, and a
helicopter."—Provided by publisher.
  ISBN 978-1-60253-148-2 (library bound : alk. paper)
  [1. Alphabet.] I. Thornburgh, Rebecca McKillip, ill. II. Title.
PZ7.M739Myh 2009
[E]—dc22   2008033164

A NOTE TO PARENTS AND EDUCATORS:

Magic moon machines and five fat frogs are just a few of the fun things you can share with children by reading books with them. Reading aloud helps children in so many ways! It introduces them to new words, motivates them to develop their own reading skills, and expands their attention span and listening abilities. So it's important to find time each day to share a book or two . . . or three!

As you read with young children, you can help develop their understanding of how print works by talking about the parts of the book—the cover, the title, the illustrations, and the words that tell the story. As you read, use your finger to point to each word, modeling a gentle sweep from left to right.

Simple word games help develop important prereading skills, including an understanding of rhyme and alliteration (when words share the same beginning sound, such as "six" and "sand"). Try playing with words from a book you've just shared: "What other words start with the same sound as moon?" "Cat and hat, do those words rhyme?" The possibilities are endless—and so are the rewards!

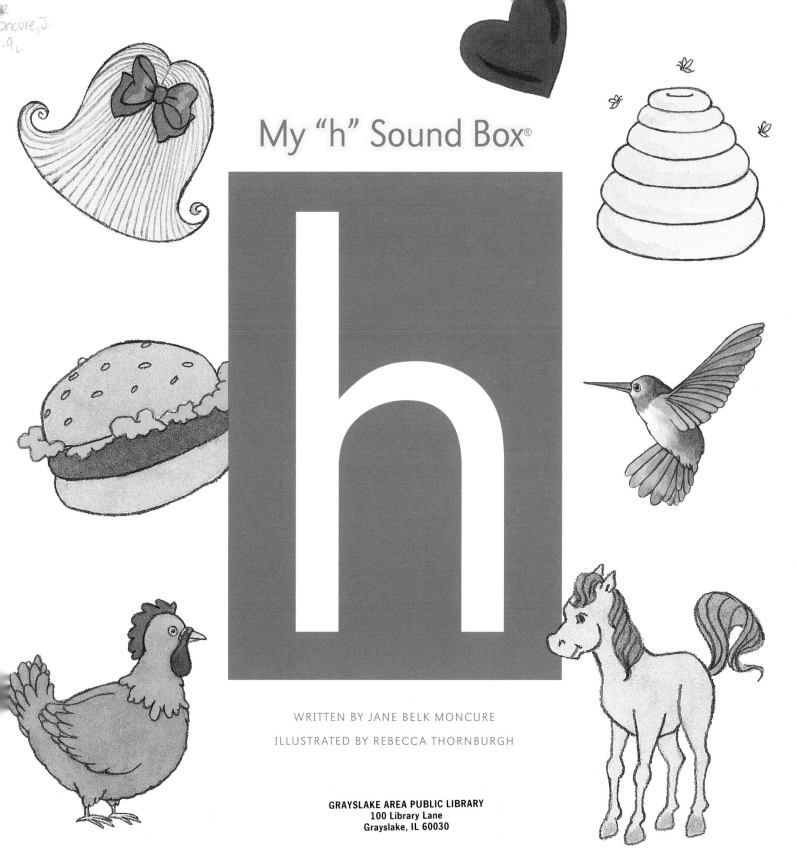

My "h" Sound Box®

h

WRITTEN BY JANE BELK MONCURE

ILLUSTRATED BY REBECCA THORNBURGH

Little 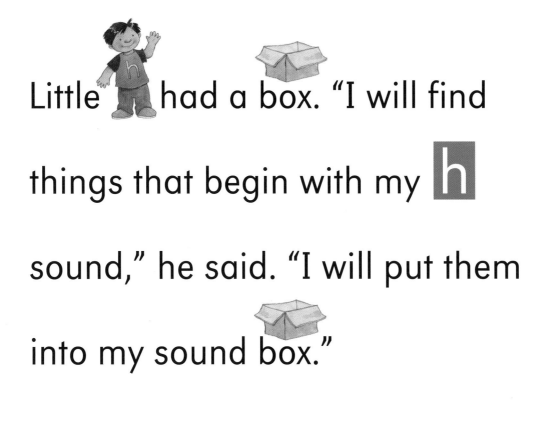 had a box. "I will find things that begin with my **h** sound," he said. "I will put them into my sound box."

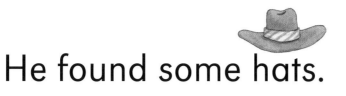

He found some hats.

He put a hat on his head. Did

he put the other hats into the

box? He did.

Little  found a hen.

"Hello," he said. "I need a hen  for my sound box." He put the hen into the box with the hats.

Then he found a hog.  Did he put the hog into the box with the hen and the hats? He did.

Little  found a horse. He

was happy. He hopped on the

horse.

He rode the  horse up a high hill.

"I want to go higher," said Little  .

But the horse could not go

higher. They were on top of the hill.

So Little  put the horse

into the box with the hats, the

hen, and the hog.

Then he found a helicopter.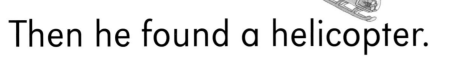

"Now I can go very high," he

said. "Higher than a hill."

The helicopter went so high that the hen, the hog, and the  horse cried, "Help! Help!" So Little put the helicopter into the box.

Now the box was heavy. Little  put it on his head. He did not see the hole.

He hopped into the hole.

"Help! Help!"

"How can we get out of this  hole?" asked the hen, the hog, and the horse.

Little  had a horn. "I will blow

my horn," he said. He blew the

horn.

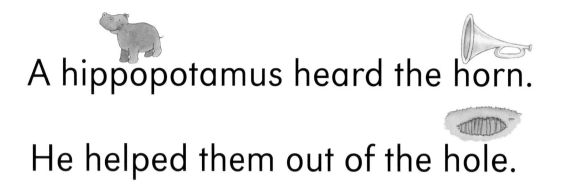

A hippopotamus heard the horn.

He helped them out of the hole.

"Hooray for the hippo!"

everyone hollered.

"How can I thank you for helping us 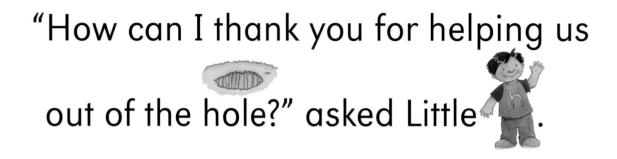 out of the hole?" asked Little 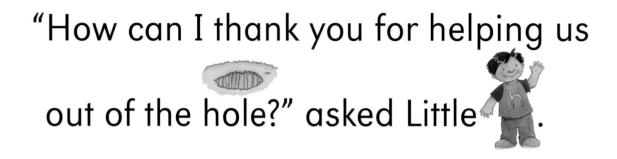.

"You can take me for a ride  in the helicopter," said the hippopotamus.

So Little  took the helicopter

out of the box. He and all the

animals went for a ride.

They flew over a highway, over a hill, and all the way home.

There, Little  spread out

his things.

My! How many he had!

Little 's Word List

hat

head

helicopter

hen

highway

hill

hippopotamus

hog

hole

home

horn

horse

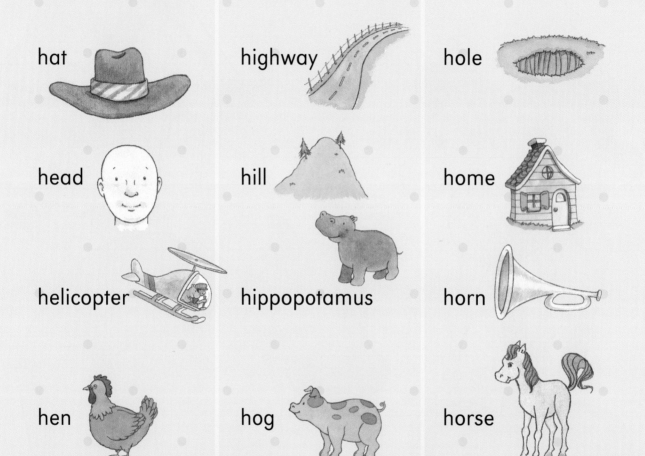

Other Words with Little

hair

hamburger

hammer

hand

harp

heart

hive

honey

hood

hospital

hot dog

hummingbird

More to Do!

 Little put hats in his box. You can collect hats, too!

Directions:

Look around your house and gather all the hats you find.

1. Sort the hats according to color. How many red hats do you have? How many purple hats do you have?

2. Sort the hats according to size. How many big hats do you have? How many little hats do you have?

Do you think the hippo, the horse, the hen, and the hog would each like to wear a hat? Which of your hats would they put on their heads?

Gather some paper and crayons. Then draw a picture of a hippo, a horse, a hen, or a hog wearing one of your hats.

31

About the Author

Best-selling author Jane Belk Moncure has written over 300 books throughout her teaching and writing career. After earning a Master's degree in Early Childhood Education from Columbia University, she became one of the pioneers in that field. In 1956, she helped form the Virginia Association for Early Childhood Education, which established the first statewide standards for teachers of young children.

Inspired by her work in the classroom, Mrs. Moncure's books have become standards in primary education, and her name is recognized across the country. Her success is reflected not only in her books' popularity with parents, children, and educators, but also by numerous awards, including the 1984 C. S. Lewis Gold Medal Award.

About the Illustrator

Rebecca Thornburgh lives in a pleasantly spooky old house in Philadelphia. If she's not at her drawing table, she's reading—or singing with her band, called Reckless Amateurs. Rebecca has one husband, two daughters, and two silly dogs.